Peppa Pig

and the

Lost Christmas List

First paperback edition 2014

Library of Congress Cataloging-in-Publication Data is available.

Library of Congress Catalog Card Number 2012942270
ISBN 978-0-7636-6276-9 (hardcover)
ISBN 978-0-7636-7456-4 (paperback)

14 15 16 17 18 19 SCP 10 9 8 7 6 5 4 3 2 1

Printed in Humen, Dongguan, China

This book was typeset in Peppa.
The illustrations were created digitally.

Candlewick Entertainment
An imprint of Candlewick Press
99 Dover Street
Somerville, Massachusetts 02144

visit us at www.candlewick.com

Peppa Pig and the Lost Christmas List

CANDLEWICK
ENTERTAINMENT

It's almost Christmas,

and Peppa Pig and her little brother, George,
are mailing their letters to Santa.
Peppa's friends are there too!

"What are you asking for?" asks Peppa.

"I'd like a **scooter**!"
says Suzy.

"I've asked Santa for a
toy spaceship!"
says Danny.

"A **toy mouse**
for me, please,"
says Emily.

Rebecca wants a **trumpet**,

Zoe has asked Santa for a **ball-and-paddle toy**,

and Candy is hoping for a **jump rope**.

Pedro would like a **guitar**.

The next day,

Mummy and Daddy Pig, Peppa, and George go to Miss Rabbit's farm to find the perfect Christmas tree.

000

They look at little ones.

"Bigger!"

says Daddy Pig.

They look at

medium-size ones.

"Bigger!"

says Daddy Pig.

The tree is very big.

Daddy Pig's car is quite small.

"No worries. I'll carry it home!" he says.

Peppa, George, and Mummy Pig
wait a very long time for Daddy Pig.
Finally they see him coming slowly up the hill.
Daddy Pig needs a rest!

It's time to decorate! Mummy Pig puts the lights on first.

Peppa adds the garland.

George hangs some Christmas ornaments.

Then Daddy Pig reaches way up high to put a star on the top.

The tree is beautiful!

Peppa sings a Christmas-tree song:

"Little star on the Christmas tree,

twinkle, twinkle, twinkle.

All the little pigs on Christmas Eve

go oink, oink, oink!"

"Daddy," asks Peppa,
"why does Santa come down the chimney?
Why doesn't he just use the front door?"

"Good question, Peppa!
If you see him, you should ask.
But Santa won't come unless you're asleep,
so up to bed you go!"

"George, let's stay awake
all night and see Santa!"
Peppa says.

But George is fast asleep.

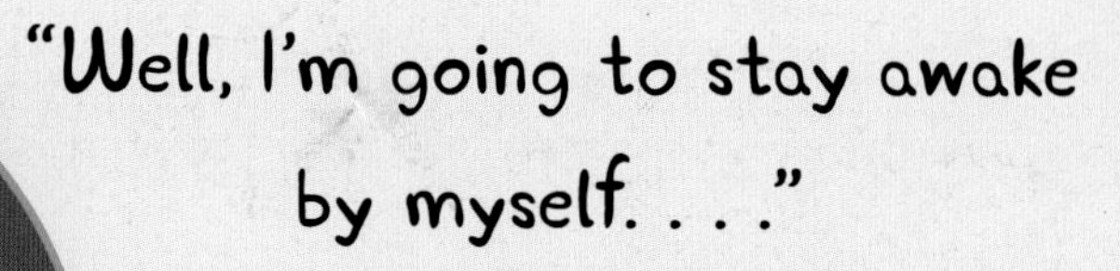

"Well, I'm going to stay awake
by myself. . . ."

Soon Peppa is fast asleep too.

THUMP!

"Ho, ho—uh-oh!

It's windy up here!"

Santa checks his list and then
squeezes down the chimney. It's a tight fit!

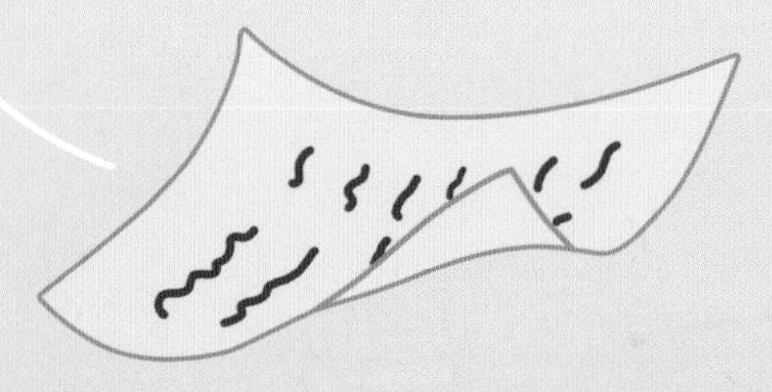

Santa is surprised to see two little pigs.

"It's me, Peppa! This is my little brother, George."

"I am very pleased to meet you," says Santa.

"Are those our presents?" asks Peppa.

"They might be. But you'll have to wait until morning to find out!"

"Santa, how do you know what presents to give everyone?" asks Peppa.

"Well, I have a list.
It's right here—oh! It *was* right here. Oh, dear.
What has happened to my list? I've lost it!
How will I know who gets which presents?"

"I can help!" says Peppa.

Danny wants a **toy spaceship**,

Emily a **toy mouse**.

A **scooter**, please, for Suzy.

Rebecca would like a **trumpet**.

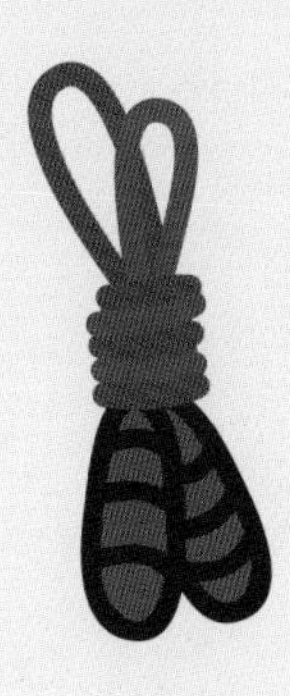

Candy wants a **jump rope**.

Zoe asked for a

ball-and-paddle toy.

And Pedro would like a **guitar**!

"Thank you, Peppa Pig!" says Santa.
"You remembered everything on the lost
Christmas list. You've saved the day! I must
hurry now." Santa looks up the chimney. "Hmmm,
I guess I'll have to squeeze up there again."

"Why don't you use the front door?"
asks Peppa.

"By golly, what a good idea!"

"Ho, ho, ho!"

On Christmas morning,
Mummy Pig and Daddy Pig wake
Peppa and George.

"Daddy, Mummy, we saw Santa!"
says Peppa. "And look, he left us presents!"

George has a **toy train**.
Peppa has a **yo-yo**.

Peppa's friends arrive.

They got the presents they asked for too!

Merry Christmas!